# CONTENTS

# A very warm welcome to my waterways world.

I'm the narrowboat Muddy Waters and I live, with many of my boat friends, on the Oxford Canal in the heart of England.

As you are about to discover, we have many adventures in very beautiful and interesting places. I have to be very careful though as I'm always on the lookout for Ol' One Eye, that nasty pirate boat. He thinks I've stolen some gold and treasure from him and he believes I know where it is. Thankfully, my friends soon let me know if he's around, **'Don't they, Jolly?'**

# 'Yes we do, Muddy,

and we know it wasn't you who stole his rotten treasure!'

This is my young friend Jolly Boatman, and he lives alongside me on the canal. He's a narrowboat too, not a barge as he's sometimes called.

'No, Muddy, I'm **not** a barge,

and never will be! The others say a barge is just
**a fat narrowboat.'**

'**Now, now,** Jolly, it's best to
just ignore those who think that. Barges
are very important boats on the waterways.
It's not their fault that they're too wide for
the Oxford Canal.'

As you can see, we narrowboats have many
important things to consider as we cruise
from town to town. And if you're curious,
you'll discover that it can sometimes be
dangerous too. **'Isn't it, Jolly?'**

'**Oh, Muddy,**

please don't tell that story. Tell them
about Hamish, or Milly, or Dudley, or...'

'**Or you?**

I think it's time we found out more about
*you* in, **'Jolly Boatman's Lesson.'**

A JOYFUL JOLLY RUSHES AHEAD,
NOW, WHAT WAS IT THAT MUDDY SAID...?

# JOLLY BOATMAN'S LESSON

I'm only small, and sometimes tiny,
I'm on every page, can you find me?....

# 'I'm bored,'

complained Jolly Boatman
to his old friend Muddy Waters.
'All the other boats have lots
to do, but I don't.'

'Why don't you help Cedric unload
his cargo?' asked Muddy. 'He is always
asking if anyone will take his loads.'

# 'But he's dirty and smelly and rude.

Anyway, Coal Face is helping
him now. They won't want me
over there.'

Muddy had a better idea. 'You and
Poppy can help get the wharf ready
for Hamish's visit. He will be here in
a few days and he'll need an extra
large mooring kept clear. Can you
do that?'

They soon had Thrupp Wharf ready for Hamish. Jolly was quickly bored again. He pestered Muddy for another job.

Bump
Bump
Bump

'Can I go down to Wolvercote to fetch the gas bottles, Muddy?' Muddy frowned. 'Please, Muddy, I know I can do it on my own now,

# please, please, please.'

Jolly bumped around Muddy pleading to be allowed to go.

'I will let you go on two conditions,' said Muddy Waters sternly.

**First,** you must carry no more than five gas bottles. **Secondly,** you must not go into the Duke's Lock. You know the River Thames can be dangerous for a lone narrowboat.'

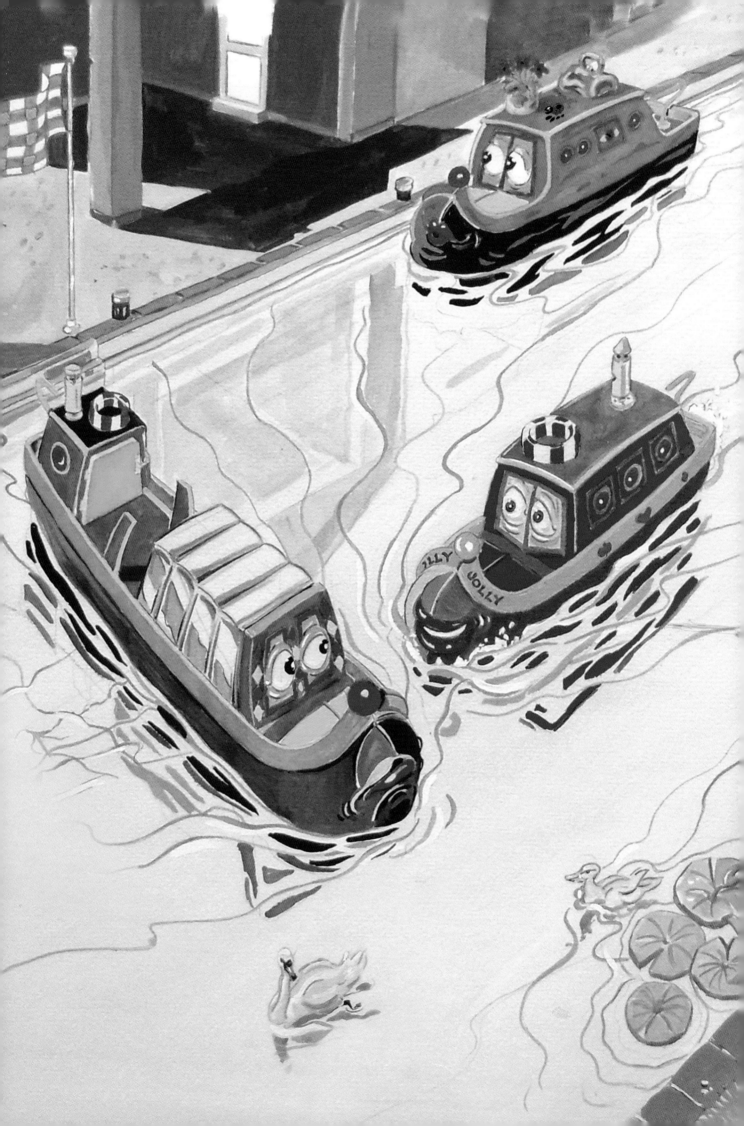

'I can carry more than five bottles,
Muddy, you know I can and I won't
go into Duke's Lock, I promise.'

'No more than five gas bottles,' insisted
Muddy as he nudged Jolly into the wharf.
'And don't be back late, we've still got
a lot to do before Hamish arrives...'

Before Muddy could finish his sentence,

Jolly was off at top speed, heading to wolvercote.

Jolly soon arrived at Wolvercote. The little narrowboat treasured his visits to the wharf. He loved the hustle and bustle that always seemed to be around. Today was his turn to be part of it.

'I've come for the gas bottles,' he announced grandly. His hold was already open and ready to take on the heavy bottles of gas. Jolly knew he could easily carry ten, but Muddy's instructions had been very clear.

'No more than five, that's all we need,'

he shouted to Larry the loader.

In no time at all he found himself at Duke's Lock, where he began to wonder what all the fuss was about. He had always been curious about the journey from the canal into the River Thames and had often asked to go.

He longed to see Wolvercote Meadow and pass through Godstow Lock. Many of the other boats had told him about their wonderful adventures on the river and how very different it was to the canal.

# I could just have a quick peep,

he thought to himself.

Jolly soon found himself through the lock. The river was high and flowing very hard. It pushed him along faster than he'd ever been. He whistled excitedly as he hurried forward. He didn't realise how much peril he was in.

He could hear the wind rushing past him. The SWOOSH of the river below made him want to go even faster.

**Suddenly,** he realised that he would need to slow down and wondered how he was going to do it. It was easy on the canal, he just reversed his engines and he came to a stop, but here..?

He put his engine into reverse. It spluttered and coughed, fighting hard against the fast flowing water, but he kept flying forwards.

'I need to **turn,**
I need to **turn,**'

he shouted.

In a desperate attempt to stop, Jolly dropped his main anchor. He felt it hit and scrabble along the riverbed. It slowed him enough to turn him side on as he headed rapidly towards the hazardous 'Trout Inn' weir.

He struggled against the powerful current, but gradually began to ease his way around.

His anchor was now fixed to the riverbed. He was using all his power and strength just to stay still. Water was coming into the hold and he wondered just how long he could last.

He let out a **desperate whistle** which seemed to drift into the air.

He'd always felt safe on the canal with lots of friends around to help. Here, he was alone and afraid. He didn't understand the powerful force that was trying to push him over the edge.

Muddy Waters was feeling very sturdy with his new engine operating at full power. He soon found himself at Godstow Lock, when he thought he heard a familiar whistle.

That's strange, he thought to himself, it sounds like Jolly's whistle. It seems to be very close and coming from the river side, not the canal.

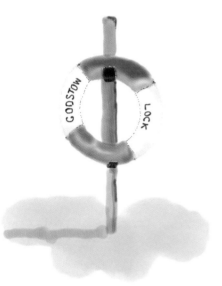

Muddy knew that Jolly should have been much further along the canal by now. **Suddenly,** the whistle came again, only this time

# louder and more urgent.

Muddy was certain that it was Jolly Boatman and that **he was in trouble.**

**splutter splutter**

Muddy could feel the flowing water pushing him backwards. His new and powerful engine drew him closer to the struggling, spluttering Jolly Boatman. He gave a loud blast on his horn letting Jolly know that help was nearby.

DANGER

As the water filled his hull, Jolly was finding it harder and harder to fight against the current. His fuel was almost exhausted. He was being pulled ever closer to the weir when he heard Muddy's blast.

'I must hold on, I must hold on'

he told himself.

Muddy rushed towards the weir. He was determined to stop Jolly drifting any closer to the danger area. He was shocked to feel the force of the river driving him to the edge.

Using every drop of the power in his

# thumping engines, he slowly pushed Jolly away from danger.

Smoke billowed from the narrowboats as they strained to escape the pull of the current. Gradually, they emerged further away from the dangerous weir. An exhausted Jolly cut away his anchor. He floated alongside a grim-faced Muddy Waters, who now had the younger boat very firmly in tow.

# 'Thank you so much for rescuing me, Muddy,'

said Jolly weakly.

## 'I'm SO sorry

I didn't listen to you,
I just wanted to have a little look.'
A large tear fell into the water.

'I know you didn't mean to get
into trouble, Jolly, but you must learn
to keep your promises,' said a weary
Muddy. 'And you must listen to boats
that care about you. We just want
to keep you safe.'

'I really have learned my lesson,
Muddy,' he said. 'And 'I'll never cut
through Duke's Lock again...' Muddy
didn't want to stop Jolly's fun, but
he would make sure that future river
trips were never taken alone.

'Let's get you back to Thrupp and
have that nasty crack in your hull seen to,
your engine will need some attention too.
Once we're home we'll soon have you

# ship shape again.'

Jolly was very pleased to be heading back to his home on the canal. Exhausted from his ordeal, he closed his eyes, happy to be safe and secure under Muddy's skilled navigation.

APPEARS IN EVERY STORY · Muddy · APPEARS IN EVERY STORY

In his early years Muddy Waters carried high value cargo such as gold and silver.

He is **very trustworthy** and the **wisest** narrowboat on the **British waterways.**

He can be relied upon to solve the most difficult problems and isn't afraid of a hard day's work.

Although he has magic in his hull he rarely uses it, preferring to rely on his own experiences.

## Other Muddy Adventures

**Muddy features in every story** but has his own special adventure in An Ice Surprise for Muddy.

MUDDY WATERS®

AN ICE SURPRISE FOR MUDDY

Written by D H Clacher © 2010. Illustrations by Stephen Preedy

| NAME: | MUDDY WATERS |
|---|---|
| Built: | 1810s |
| Hull: | Wooden |
| Size: | 69ft / 21m |
| Role: | Cargo carrier |
| Special Powers: | Mystic abilities |
| Base: | Thrupp, Oxfordshire |
| Weight: | 40 Tonnes |
| Engine: | 2 x 60hp Diesel |

One of the oldest cargo carriers around, he's known and loved by most, but not all, other boats.

An ancient feud between him and Ol' One Eye continues with the nasty pirate boat always looking for revenge.

Muddy's home is on the Oxford Canal with his friends, Jolly Boatman, Poppy, Dizzy Spells and Cedric the Dredger.

MUDDY'S TRAVELS

OPENED IN 2002 SCOTLAND

The Falkirk Wheel

The Anderton Boat Lift

OPENED IN 1875 ENGLAND

OPENED IN 1805 WALES

The Pontcysyllte Aqueduct

# JOLLY BOATMAN

THE YOUNGEST BOAT IN MUDDY WATERS

Jolly

**Jolly Boatman was built in Heyford Wharf on the Oxford Canal.**

This is a busy boatyard where new boats are made and others are repaired.

Jolly is young for a boat. The older boats at Thrupp are there to guide and teach him, especially Muddy Waters.

# He is **keen** to learn about the world but **does rush** things.

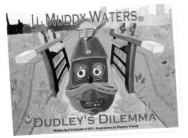

**JOLLY IN A JOT**

| NAME: | JOLLY BOATMAN |
|---|---|
| Built: | 1950s |
| Hull: | Steel |
| Size: | 39ft / 12m |
| Role: | Apprentice (learning) |
| Special Powers: | None |
| Base: | Thrupp, Oxfordshire |
| Weight: | 15 Tonnes |
| Engine: | 30hp Single diesel |

## Other Jolly Adventures

**Find out more about him in** Dudley's Dilemma and...

...Midsummer Milly.

He has many adventures throughout the Muddy Waters stories. Hopefully, he will use these experiences to learn how to be a good working boat.

**BEST FRIENDS**

You'll find Jolly alongside Muddy in every one of the Muddy Waters tales.

HELPED BUILD THE ICONIC LONDON EYE

Pearly

## Pearly has always lived and worked in London.

He knows the city very well and is known to be water wise. He is always on hand to guide lost boats. He loves the hustle and bustle of the busy docks, as well as the wide and colourful range of boats he sees every day.

He is very proud of his role in the building of the London Eye. He was one of the team of boats chosen to carry the heavy pods across the Thames. He forgets to tell other boats that he nearly lost a pod for the Eye, by going too fast through the very choppy water!

As a young boat he was given a golden **'P' for Pearly** which he wears with pride.

He is also full of mischief and this often gets him into trouble. He is Jolly's older cousin and we learn more about him when Jolly makes his first visit to the city, in 'Pearly's Welcome to London'.

# A **cheerful** and **popular** character, **Pearly** is very **proud** of his home.

**PEARLY'S POINTS**

### Other Pearly Adventures

**Find out more about him in** Pearly's Welcome to London.

| NAME: | PEARLY WHITES |
|---|---|
| Built: | 1930s |
| Hull: | Steel |
| Size: | 39ft / 12m |
| Role: | Odd jobs, light cargo |
| Special Powers: | None |
| Base: | River Thames, London |
| Weight: | 18 Tonnes |
| Engine: | 50hp Single diesel |

# DIZZY SPELLS

DIZZY SPELLS

DIZZY • IS KIND AND HELPFUL • IS KIND AND HELPFUL • IS KIND AND HELPFUL •

**Dizzy was made and trained in a magic boatyard.**

She wasn't a top student as she found it hard to concentrate. She only just passed her final exams. Her forgetfulness gets her into trouble, but everyone loves her.

Fin of fish and knot of rope, mix them well with a pinch of hope.

Her first spell

| NAME: | DIZZY SPELLS |
|---|---|
| Built: | 1890s |
| Hull: | Wooden |
| Size: | 39ft / 12m |
| Role: | Problem solver |
| Special Powers: | Magic skills |
| Base: | Thrupp, Oxfordshire |
| Weight: | 30 Tonnes |
| Engine: | 25hp Single diesel |

She is kind and tries hard to help, but things don't always go as planned! Her spell for sunny weather went badly wrong and caused **huge** floods instead.

'Fin of fish and knot of rope, mix them well with a pinch of hope' was Dizzy's spell, but it should have been:

'Tongue of frog and a duck tail feather, stir up quick for warm sunny weather!'

Her *great strength* is her knowledge of the natural world, stars and planets.

This often balances out her wayward spells.

## Other Dizzy Adventures

**Find out more about her in** Poppy at the Boat Show and...

...Ol' One Eye's Revenge.

# IT'S MUDDY IN AMERICA

On a bright summer's day, Muddy Waters, Jolly Boatman and Dizzy Spells were busy at Thrupp Wharf in Oxford. Muddy Waters had something very special to tell Jolly.

 'Well, Jolly, it's time for our **biggest adventure yet**.'

 '**WOW!** Are we going back to Scotland, or Wales, or...?'

 'Not this time, Jolly. This time we're **going much further**.'

 'That's right, Jolly. We're actually going to... **America!**'

 'You've gone very quiet, Jolly. Did you hear Dizzy, we're going to see our friends **in the USA?**'

'I did hear, Muddy, but that means we have to cross the ocean and I'm just a little narrowboat.'

'**Oh, Jolly,** you don't need to worry about that.'

'**But I am worried, Muddy.** It's so far and... Oh, I see, is Dizzy going to use her magic to get us there?'

'What a **wonderful idea,** Jolly. I'm sure I could easily find a spell to get us over there. Now, let me see...'

'**That's very kind** of you, Dizzy, but I think we'll find another way. We all know how wayward your spells can be sometimes.'

'**So, how** will we get over there, Muddy?'

'Let's head to **London,** where all will be revealed.'

Join us on this epic voyage and find out what happens next in, **'IT'S MUDDY IN AMERICA.'**

AMERICA CALLS OUR ADVENTUROUS CREW,
TO TRAVEL ITS WATERS AND MAKE FRIENDS ANEW.

# IT'S MUDDY IN AMERICA

Don't forget to look and see,
on each page, where I might be……

# The **big day** arrived at last.

Muddy Waters and his dear friends, Jolly Boatman and Dizzy Spells, were off to America. He had been invited to visit his cousins in New York and hoped they would arrive in time to take part in the famous Hudson River Races.

Big Ted, the cargo ship, reassured a very excited but nervous Jolly about the long trip across the Atlantic Ocean. 'You'll be safe with me,' he boomed.

'It's time for the open seas!'

TOOT
TOOT
TOOT

The narrowboats felt very important indeed when they saw the gates of Tower Bridge in London raised.

# 'They put them up just for us!'

shouted an excited Jolly Boatman.

Everyone tooted and whistled as the explorers headed off on their longest ever adventure.

TOOT TOOT

Out in the Atlantic Ocean, the enormous waves took everyone by surprise.

# Big Ted had never seen such huge icebergs before.

He used all his strength and skill to avoid them.

# 'Hold on folks,'

he bellowed above the roar of the wind and rain. A wide eyed Jolly was gripped tightly between Dizzy and Muddy. Ted battled to keep them safe, but the journey took longer than usual.

Arriving late, the exhausted crew
were thrilled by the reception
waiting for them in

# New York
# Harbor.

Hello

Welcome

Hello

Howdy

Welcome

Friendly fireboats sprayed their special welcome all around. Even the majestic Statue of Liberty wanted to say **hello!**

Chip, Liberty Belle, Libby to her friends, and Soda Sam were thrilled to finally meet their English visitors. They hurried into the harbour, impatient to greet their new friends.

# There was no time to lose.

The Hudson River Races couldn't go ahead without Chip's special cargo and the American boats were eager to be on their way.

Ted was very proud to deliver the boats safely to their American friends.

# There was lots of whooping and whistling

and everyone seemed to speak at once. Jolly had to listen very hard to the American boats, as he'd never heard voices like theirs before.

'They do talk strangely,' he whispered to Muddy Waters.

'They'll be thinking the same about you too, Jolly,' laughed Muddy.

Libby explained that Chip had a precious and fragile load to deliver to the yearly races. 'They can't start the show without me,' announced Chip grandly.

'We need to move fast, we can chat as we go,' urged Libby. She knew that storms were in the air. Her greatest fear, however was that

# Thunderguts, a mean and nasty ship

would be waiting for them.

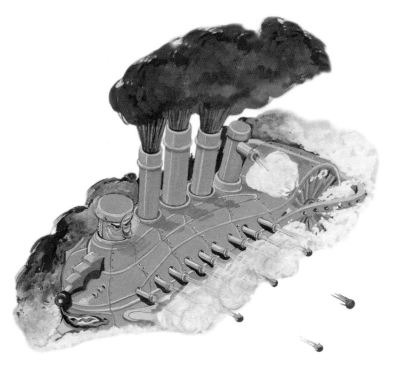

He was known to attack any boat that strayed into his water. Dizzy felt the American boats seemed rather nervous.

Further upriver, everyone was getting to know each other. Jolly and Sam argued about which of them was the fastest boat. Soda Sam was very sure he would beat Jolly at the races.

'WOW, you got a ladybug on your nose, Jolly,' said Soda Sam.

'That's not a **Ladybug,**' replied Jolly indignantly. 'It's a **Ladybird.**'

'Lady**bug**,' argued Sam.

'Ladybird!' insisted Jolly.

'Well, its the strangest **bird** I ever did see,' laughed Sam.

The next day, under darkening
skies, the crew continued
at full speed upriver.

'We need to be careful
on this stretch,'
said Libby.

She didn't want to worry her new friends, but she knew that Thunderguts, the mean old ironclad boat, patrolled nearby.

# Danger lurked

around every corner on this part of the river. **They had to move fast...**

**Suddenly,** there was an almighty roaring and growling.

Thunderguts sped towards the terrified boats.

Grrrrrr

Grrrr

Roar

ROar
ROar

His cannons were blazing and thick black smoke leapt from his huge funnels. He vowed to sink and destroy any boat that entered his territory. Easy pickings, he thought as he **steamed noisily ahead.**

# 'This is **my** water!'

boomed Thunderguts.

# 'You'll pay for trespassing!'

he hissed.

**Cannon balls struck** a terrified Muddy, Jolly and Sam as they tried desperately to help Chip escape. Despite being injured, the little boats were too fast for a lumbering Thunderguts as they scattered across the river. Chip took his chance to get away unnoticed.

Their joy at outrunning the old steamer didn't last long as they sailed headlong into even greater danger.

Rain fell heavily as dark clouds closed all around them. The air was thick with cannon smoke, lit only by blinding flashes of lightning. Each boat

**rolled** and **swayed** as waves of water **battered** them.

They were tired, confused and hopelessly lost. Libby peered through the smoke and gloom, relieved to make out the friendly beam of a nearby lighthouse. **'Over here,'** she called. 'We'll soon be out of this storm.'

Thanks to Libby the
boats made it to safety.
Chip was so happy to see
that they had all escaped.

'Now that was
too close
for comfort,'

he said as he stared at their injuries. They
all agreed heartily, relieved to be safe from
the storm and the very mean Thunderguts.

'The river races start tomorrow. Now, Chip is that
box still in one piece?' asked Libby nervously.

'Sure is!' replied a thankful but weary Chip.

Dizzy spent the day mending
the boats damaged in the battle.
Now it was time for her and Jolly to

# relax and marvel at the evening's emerging fireflies.

Muddy asked Libby how she had
been able to save them all from the
storm. Glancing at Jolly and Dizzy,
she laughed adding, 'I just looked for
lights in the sky too, Muddy. On this
river the old lighthouses will always
**keep you safe.'**

The brave little boats received a heroes' welcome as they arrived at the pageant. Chip was nervous, but very proud as he carefully lowered his treasured cargo into place.

Everyone fell silent as the countdown began,

# five - four - three - two - one... BOOM!

Firecrackers and rockets filled the air as the signal to start the races.

'Phew!' cried Jolly as shivers ran through his hull, 'It looks like it's **our** turn to fill the skies with light and fire!'

# THUNDERGUTS

THUNDERGUTS

The largest boat!

THUNDERGUTS

## Thunderguts was originally a wooden sailing ship built in the USA.

During the American Civil War he was covered with armour plating.

He was also given huge cannons to carry. Although this made him more powerful, it meant he lost his special hearing powers. It also made him very slow and bad tempered.

| NAME: | THUNDERGUTS |
| --- | --- |
| Built: | 1840s |
| Hull: | Wood, covered in iron |
| Size: | HUGE! |
| Role: | Warship |
| Special Powers: | Lost |
| Base: | Hudson River, USA |
| Weight: | 200 Tonnes |
| Engine: | Half Trunk Steam 320hp |

# Thunderguts, has **never** stopped **fighting** with **anyone** he sees.

No-one has ever been able to sink him, although many have tried. Other boats try to keep out of his way.

# LIBERTY BELLE

**LIBBY'S LOT**

| NAME: | LIBERTY BELLE (LIBBY) |
|---|---|
| Built: | 1850s |
| Hull: | Wooden |
| Size: | 140ft / 43m |
| Role: | Paddle steamer |
| Special Powers: | Senses dangers |
| Base: | Hudson River, USA |
| Weight: | 110 Tonnes |
| Engine: | Steam 250hp |

CAN SENSE DANGER • Libby • CAN SENSE DANGER

**Libby was built on the Mississippi River as a leisure boat.**

She can navigate in shallow waters and against strong currents. As with Muddy, she has magic in her hull, and can sense when danger is around. She is respected by other boats.

Libby has **magic** in her hull.

| NAME: | CHIP |
|---|---|
| Built: | 1980s |
| Hull: | Steel and carbon fibre |
| Size: | 35ft / 11m |
| Role: | Experimental boat - technical |
| Special Powers: | None |
| Base: | Hudson River, USA |
| Weight | 2.5 Tonnes |
| Engine: | Twin Turbo Gas 120hp |

# CHIP

**Chip was built and shipped from California in the west.**

He is computer aided. His hull is very strong and light which makes him extremely fast.

He is very proud to have been given the job to set off the fireworks on the Hudson River.

| NAME: | SODA SAM |
|---|---|
| Built: | 1950s |
| Hull: | Steel |
| Size: | 39ft / 12m |
| Role: | To carry and advertise soda |
| Special Powers: | None |
| Base: | Hudson River, USA |
| Weight: | 5 Tonnes |
| Engine: | 4 Cylinder Gas 30hp |

# SODA SAM

**Sam was specially built to carry cans and bottles of a very well known fizzy drink (soda).**

Soda Sam is fast moving and loves to race.

79

# GLOSSARY

## Canal
Canals are waterways that have been built into the land and filled with water. They allow boats and ships to travel with their cargo and passengers from place to place.

**C**

## Cargo
Things like wood and coal carried from place to place by the boats.

## Cargo Ship
These are usually bigger boats or ships which carry very heavy loads. They are much bigger than narrowboats.

## Current
Fast moving water travelling through still water.

**D**

## Docks
A place built by the waterside for boats and ships to come to with their cargo and passengers.

**F**

## Fireflies
These are small, flying bugs which can be seen glowing at night.

## Funnels
Large tubes fitted to ships for waste gases to escape from. They are often seen on ships with smoke coming from them.

**G**

## Gas Bottles
Containers which hold the gas needed as fuel by the narrowboats.

**H**

## Hudson River lighthouses
Dating from the early 1800s, there were originally 14 lighthouses along the river. Today, a total of 7 have been preserved and are in working order.

## Hull
The main part of a boat, including the bottom, sides and deck.

**I**

## Ironclad
This was the name given to wooden warships which were covered with iron plates to protect them. They were used during the American Civil War (1861-1865).

## L

### Ladybug
The American word for ladybird, a small beetle, usually with a red or yellow body and black spots.

### Lock
Gates on the canal which can be opened or closed to change the water level. Then boats can be raised or lowered as they travel through hills and valleys.

## M

### Mooring
A space where boats can stop and be attached to the canal or riverbank with a rope.

## N

### Narrowboat
A canal boat less than 2.1 metres or 7 feet wide. It is steered with a tiller not a wheel.

### Navigation
Finding a way around and through the sea, canals and rivers.

### New York Harbor
A harbour is a place on the coast where boats can safely find shelter. Some are made by nature, but many are constructed. In America, the spelling of harbour has no u, as in New York Harbor.

## T

### Tiller
A handle fitted to the top of the rudder which is used to steer the boat.

### Tower Bridge
A famous bridge in London which has two arms which can be raised and lowered to let tall ships pass through. It was opened in 1894.

## W

### Weir
A low dam built across a river to control the flow of water.

### Wharf
A smaller place than a harbour where boats can stop to load and unload their cargo.

# MUDDY WATERS®

## Series One

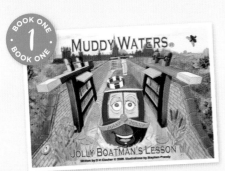

ISBN – 978-09563505-0-3

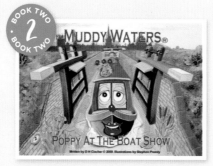

ISBN – 978-09563505-2-7

ISBN – 978-09563505-1-0

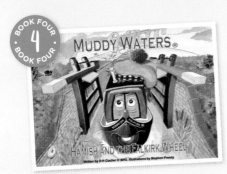

ISBN – 978-09563505-3-4

ISBN – 978-09563505-4-1

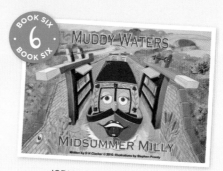

ISBN – 978-09563505-5-8

ISBN – 978-09563505-7-2

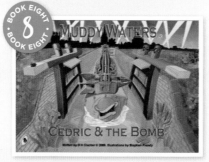

ISBN – 978-09563505-6-5

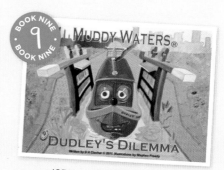

ISBN – 978-09563505-8-9

ISBN – 978-09563505-9-6

All books have 32 pages and 14 full colour, hand painted plates.
Height 148mm  Width 210mm  Spine Width 3mm  Weight 115g

### Jolly Boatman's Lesson

Muddy Waters thinks it's time to let Jolly Boatman out on his own. In this episode Jolly learns about the hazards to be found on the waterways. More importantly, he also learns the importance of keeping his promises.

 ### Poppy at the Boat Show

There's going to be a boat show and Jolly Boatman is convinced he can win. Tired old Poppy reflects on her glory years and wishes she could go too. Dizzy Spells decides something must be done, but can her wayward powers work?

 ### Pearly's Welcome to London

Muddy Waters and Jolly Boatman leave Oxford to embark on their big London adventure. Jolly hopes Pearly will look after him as he struggles in the big city, but Pearly has something far more important on his mind...

 ### Hamish and the Falkirk Wheel

Following his visit to Thrupp, Hamish leads his old friend Muddy Waters, and an excited Jolly Boatman on the long journey to Scotland. Overawed by the huge Falkirk Wheel, can Jolly overcome his fears?

 ### Ol' One Eye's Revenge

Muddy, Jolly and Dizzy head off to Gloucester Docks in search of cocoa, the ingredient that makes chocolate so delightfully yummy. But danger awaits them... Ol' One Eye and his gang lurk in the shadows, waiting for a chance to seize on the Thrupp boats. Will the pirates catch them, or will wit and wisdom prevail? Perhaps a springtime phenomenon will lend a hand too...

### Midsummer Milly

Narrowboat Milly makes the arduous journey from her beloved city of Manchester to Oxfordshire to see her friends in Thrupp. She has cracks and leaks in her hull and hopes that Old Badger at Stoke Bruerne can help her with her aches and pains. The Midsummer's Day celebrations are in full swing on the Grand Union Canal when she meets wise Old Badger. Will she get the chance of a trip through the enchanted tunnel?

 ### An Ice Surprise for Muddy

It's Muddy Waters' 200th birthday and the Thrupp boats are planning a surprise party. Keeping the preparations secret from the wise old narrowboat isn't easy. In all of the hustle and bustle Dawn Chorus' warning of an impending storm is ignored. With the ice and snow closing in on the canal, will Muddy ever get to his party at Tooley's Boatyard?

 ### Cedric and the Bomb

Whilst dredging the Oxford Canal Cedric uncovers a WWII bomb which he almost tips into Coal Face's hold. With his wartime experiences very much in mind, Cedric knows what must be done. Can the Thrupp crew help the rude old dredger out of his fix, or is there going to be final big bang for Cedric? Find out in this touch and go waterways drama.

 ### Dudley's Dilemma

Muddy and friends are off to see Dudley in Birmingham. He's being given a very special waterways award for his hard work. He helps the Oxfordshire boats to deliver their precious cargo of cocoa to the chocolate factory, but soon realises that Jolly Boatman is missing somewhere in the myriad of the city's canals. Does Dudley leave the other boats to find Jolly or does he press on to pick up his prize?

 ### Owen's Dancing Dragon

Strange things have been seen on the Pontcysyllte Aqueduct. There have been sightings of Dragons breathing fire and flying through the night. Many boats are too scared to cross the 200 year old waterway, but Muddy Waters and his friends are determined to investigate. Owen and Hamish cross swords in this mysterious Celtic adventure.

Find out more at
www.muddywaters.org.uk

# ACKNOWLEDGEMENTS

**A very special thank you** is owed to some inspirational and exceptional pupils and teachers at the elementary school at RAF Croughton, Oxfordshire. Ms Kathleen Whalen and all of the American pupils at the USAF base were the driving force behind the 'It's Muddy in America' story. Their enthusiasm for all things Muddy Waters made our US adventure truly come to life, as Soda Sam would no doubt agree!

The sparkling and remarkable layout of this book was produced by Jenny Lawrence, a wonderfully talented and outstanding graphic designer. Her passion for Muddy and friends shines through on every page, for which we're extremely grateful.

**Author of the popular Muddy Waters series,** Dan Clacher is passionate about Britain's beautiful waterways. Inspired by his daughter and grandsons, he's been writing for children for over a decade. On meeting Stephen Preedy, Dan knew immediately that this talented illustrator would transform his 'silly stories' into a riot of colour and life. Dan sets every tale in 'real' locations and Stephen applies his unique interpretation to every hand painted picture.

Dan and Stephen have also written and illustrated two children's books for the Rivertime Boat Trust, a charity which takes children and adults on magical trips along the River Thames.

**A huge thank you** is owed to the many people behind the success of the Muddy Waters stories. It would take another book to list every contributor and supporter, but all our friends on the Oxford Canal deserve a special mention. David Dare and the crew at Oxfordshire Narrowboats in Lower Heyford have been tireless supporters of our ventures and the inspiration behind the 'real' Muddy Waters boats appearing on the canal.

www.muddywaters.org.uk

**Printed in the United Kingdom**